SKIN

RICK JASPER

NIGHT FALL

SKIN

RICK JASPER

MINNEAPOLIS

Darby Creek
A division of Lerner Publishing Group, Inc.
241 First Avenue North
Minneapolis, MN 55401 U.S.A.

Web site address: www.lernerbooks.com

Cover design: Emily Love
Cover photograph: Photolibrary

Jasper, Rick, 1948–
Skin / by Rick Jasper.
   p.   cm. — (Night fall)
ISBN 978-0-7613-6143-5 (lib. bdg. : alk. paper)
   [1. Horror stories.]   I. Title.
PZ7.J32Sk 2010
[Fic]—dc22   2010002351

Manufactured in the United States of America
1—BP—7/15/10

For my mom,
my first writing teacher

Deep into that darkness peering, long I stood there wondering, fearing,
Doubting, dreaming dreams no mortal ever dared to dream before

—Edgar Allan Poe, The Raven

Mom buried her face in *People* while we waited in the examining room for the doctor. The nurse had seemed nice, if a little frustrated, when she was taking my temperature. She took it twice. Then she frowned at the thermometer and scribbled something down.

There was a shuffle in the hall, a pause, then a knock. The doctor came in, holding out his hand. "Hello, I'm Dr. Farmer."

Dr. Zach Farmer was younger than I'd expected. He was looking at me intently, the way doctors do. I could tell he was wondering about my sweater.

It was the warmest thing I could find, a wool cardigan Mom's last boyfriend had left at the house nine months ago. I'm sure it looked out of place. It was early fall, but the weather was still like summer.

Mom jumped up. "Good morning, doctor, I'm Lucille. I'm Nick's mother. I hope this won't take a long time." She was dying for a cigarette—it'd been half an hour since the last one. She was crazy jittery.

The doctor's eyes did something for a split second—annoyance? Then he was back to professional. "I hope so too, Mrs. Barry.

"Tell me about your skin, Nick. How long since it got serious?"

Mom broke in, "I keep telling that boy—sugar, chocolate, pizza . . . . What does he expect? Now the zits are out of control, and we have to go to the doctor! Teenagers!"

I thought about disappearing.

"Well," the doctor said, "acne is different for every person, and the connection with diet hasn't ever really been proven." Then, turning to me, "So the good news, Nick, is that this isn't your fault."

Mom retreated to her chair and her magazine. Score one for the doc.

"So when did this start?"

"Two weeks ago, maybe three."

"Does it come and go? Get worse and then get better?"

"No, it started, and it's just gotten worse."

"Do you play any sports, Nick? Any hard exercise?"

Mom rolled her eyes. OK, Mom, I thought, I'm a nerd. I read. Books. Deal with it.

I answered the question. "No."

"OK." He looked at his notes. "I see you're allergic to cats."

Mom again. "Not till a few weeks ago. Now it's more like the cat's allergic to Nick. Toby won't go near him. When Nick comes close, he hisses."

"You aren't taking any medications?"

I shook my head.

"Do you feel different, physically, since your skin broke out?"

"I feel cold."

"Chills? Shivering?"

"Cold. Like winter."

"I noticed the sweater. Do you feel cold today?"

"Yes."

"All right, let's take a look at your skin. Are you breaking out anywhere besides your face? Your chest, back, or shoulders? Usually bad acne spreads around the upper body."

"No."

He turned a bright light on my face, and I closed my eyes. For a moment he held my chin, where there were two large, oozing pimples. He felt my forehead.

"Hmmm. Your skin does feel cold. Have you been popping or scratching any of these?"

"Maybe a little."

"OK, let's look at your ears." He quickly checked my ears, nose, and throat. "Now I'm going to listen to your heart and lungs. Could you unbutton your sweater?

"Take a deep breath. Breathe out. Another breath—"

He sounded puzzled. "Have you been having any breathing problems? A cough? Wheezing?"

I shook my head.

"OK." He moved the stethoscope. "Deep breath

again . . . . OK, hold your breath for a moment . . . ."

He stopped again and frowned. Then he saw me watching him. I probably looked worried.

"It's all right," he said, like he was trying to reassure both of us. "You are breathing. It's just not a sound I've heard before. Here—" He handed me the stethoscope. "Listen for yourself."

I put the discs to my ears, not sure what to expect. What I heard made the hair on the back of my neck stand up. It sounded like people. People screaming.

My name is Nick Barry, and I'm invisible. At least I was until now. I live with my mom, who mostly doesn't see me, unless I cause a problem for her.

By "problem," I mean anything that would force her to pay any extra attention to me. As she often points out, her life is hard enough without me making it harder.

My father left when I was a baby. Mom says that she didn't know him for long. He was handsome and smart and wanted to do something with his life. He tried community college twice, but, the way my mom tells it, he spent too much time at the local casinos instead of the local library.

Mom works two jobs. During the week, she's an assistant manager at Monica's Gift Emporium. On weekends she cleans offices. When she comes home, all she wants is a steaming hot bubble bath, a fresh pack of smokes, and whatever is on the Lifetime channel. She's tired, and God forbid that something unexpected should mess up her routine. Something like me missing the bus home from school, or needing homework supplies, or the trouble I'm telling about here.

I'm a freshman at Bridgewater High School, and I've been pretty much invisible there as well. BHS is even bigger than Bridgewater Middle School. I went there three years without making a close friend or even having the same teacher twice. The popular kids, the ones who run for student council, are always giving speeches about getting involved in after-school activities. But those things mean "extra" meetings and fees, and "parental involvement is encouraged." Mom would freak.

I'm not whining. Being invisible isn't all bad. As long as I keep up with my schoolwork and do my chores, my time is my own. Since I was little I've been free to explore the town of Bridgewater and the big woods on the outskirts, near where I live.

In English class last year we could get extra credit for memorizing a poem. The one I learned had this line: "The woods are lovely, dark and deep." Now I think of that whenever I'm walking there. It sounds strange, but you can almost hear the quiet on the outskirts. Old paths, overgrown with brush and thorns, wind up and down steep hills. Black rocks, some of them taller than I am, seem to grow right out of the ground. And everywhere, running in random directions, are old, crumbling walls made of flat, gray stones.

And there's the place I call the well. It's a stone wall like the others, but it's built in a circle about six feet across. I don't know whether it really is—or was—a well. But there's water at the bottom. I've dropped pebbles in and heard them splash. There's something peaceful and eerie about that place. Sometimes I'll take a book and spend hours there.

That's where I was sitting one night, around dusk, the first time the coldness came over me. Not a shivery, goose-bumpy cold, but a cold like ice living in my bones.

Later, I was sitting by that same well when I decided to ask Mom if we could see a doctor about my skin. For two weeks I'd been hoping it would clear up on its own. I'd used my lunch money to buy some zit cream at the drugstore. I followed all the directions, but it just got worse. And everything I could find online said the same thing: If it doesn't work, see your doctor.

After all my years of being invisible, kids at school were starting to notice me. Passing them in the hall, I'd notice them staring. Once a group of girls who thought I couldn't hear them whispered, "Eeuww!"

I waited till Mom was relaxed in front of the TV. Then I waited for a commercial.

"Mom, my skin's breaking out really bad."

She continued looking at the screen. "You're a teenager, Nick. You get pimples. Keep your face clean, watch what you eat."

"I've been doing that, and it's not helping. I think I need to see a doctor."

A deep sigh. "A doctor for pimples? He'll tell you the same thing I just said and charge me for it. What's he going to do, send you to the zit hospital?"

"Mom, look at me!"

"It's been a hard day, Nick. I just want to . . ."

"Please, look at me!"

And she did. And her eyes got a little wider, like those kids I passed in the hall. "Does it hurt?" she asked.

"No, but it's getting worse."

Another sigh. I was officially a problem. "OK. I don't know how we'll afford it, but I'll make an appointment. I'll use my lunch hour."

And that's how I wound up at the doctor's. That's how I wound up hearing a strange noise coming from my own body. A noise that sounded like people trapped in a very crowded part of hell.

The doctor was watching me. "Pretty weird, huh?"

"Uh huh." I gave him back his stethoscope.

"But no trouble breathing?"

"No."

"OK. Just to be sure, we're going to do a chest X-ray."

Mom hadn't seemed to be paying attention. Now you could have heard her groan across the hall. "Doctor, we have to pay for this! I don't have insurance. Nick has pimples! You can see that without an X-ray!"

"We just need to do a couple of tests to make sure Nick doesn't have any problems besides his complexion. A lot of our patients have limited funds. We won't charge you more than you can afford."

"I'll meet you at the car, Mom," I said, giving her a "go away" look.

She sighed and headed up the hall, digging in her purse for cigarettes.

The nurse came in and took blood from my right arm. I had to go down the hall and pee in a cup. When I came back, the doctor and the nurse were discussing my case.

She: "I know it's impossible, but that's what it said."

He: "Take it again, OK? Maybe it wasn't in long enough."

She: "It beeped."

The doctor looked at me. "Nick, this is Cindy. She's going to take your temperature one more time. Then we'll get that X-ray."

Three minutes later he was back. "It was the same, doctor," Cindy said. "95.8."

The doctor frowned. "Wow. Well, Nick, you said you were cold, right?"

I nodded.

"All the time?"

"Sometimes." I thought about that day in the woods. "It comes and goes."

He motioned me to follow him, and we went through a door that said "Radiology." He told me to take off my sweater and shirt. The nurse sat me on a high chair next to a panel on the wall and put a lead apron on my lap.

"OK," the doctor said. "Press your chest against that panel in front of you. Take a deep breath and hold it."

A quick buzzing sound and it was over. They told me I could put my clothes back on. I was just putting an arm in my shirt when the doctor said, "Wait a minute, Nick." He was looking at my chest. "Looks like you've got a little rash or something."

It was something. Not so much a rash as a line of faint scratch marks. I would have thought Toby made them—he often scratches a little when I pet him—but Toby hadn't come near me in weeks. The funny thing was that the scratch marks looked almost like writing.

"Do you ever scratch yourself?" the doctor asked.

"You mean like cutting? No way."

He felt the surface of the scratches and shrugged. They were faint. The writing thing was probably my imagination.

"All right, you can get dressed," he said.

Then Cindy appeared with a regular camera. "The blemishes on your face are probably acne, Nick," the doctor said. "But they're a little different from what I usually see. I'm going to send some photos to a friend who's an expert in dermatology, or skin diseases. We'll see what he says. We'll have results of your tests in a week or so. I'm sending you with some samples of a cream for your face. Here's my card. If things don't get better in three days, call me."

It was Thursday. In three days, things would definitely not be better.

grabbed my gut and doubled over when the fist hit my stomach. At the same time, someone was grabbing me, trying to force me to the ground. People were shouting. I punched out blindly with my right fist and heard a yelp as something crunched under my knuckles. Then the whistle was blowing, and the weight on my back suddenly wasn't there.

"Knock it off!" a voice screamed. "Stay where you are and don't move!"

I opened my eyes. There was blood on my hand and the front of my shirt. Coach Tyree had a headlock on Stevie Furman, who was blowing bubbles of blood and snot from his nose. Jack Stenson, all two hundred pounds of him, stood off to the side, glaring at me. Cowering to the side, looking like he was trying not to cry, was Eric Timothy.

"Get up, Barry!" Coach yelled. "Everybody! You're all seeing Blackstreet! Now!"

The fight had started with Eric. That it was a fight, and not just another chance for Jack to torment the "girly boy," was probably my fault.

I'm not friends with Eric. I'm not really friends with anyone. But Jack Stenson is a disease. He's been a bully since kindergarten. Now he seems to have chosen torturing the weak as a career.

Eric, in this case, fit the role of "the weak." Thin, blond, and hyper. He wasn't much of a student, except in music. He played violin every year at the school holiday concert. I'm no judge, but I'd heard adults say he was very, very good. Eric stuttered a little, but he was OK to talk to if you wanted to talk about Mozart or Bach or Beethoven. He kind of lit up then. It made you happy to see that, because the rest of his life didn't look that great.

Stenson can smell guys like Eric the way a shark can smell blood. It was at the end of gym class when I saw Stenson jacking Eric up against a locker. I should have ignored it. Everyone else did. But when I heard the stuff he was saying, and saw Eric look helplessly in my direction, I couldn't just do nothing.

Right by Stenson, as always, was his slave, Stevie Furman (rhymes with *vermin*). Little Stevie had as many victim qualities as Eric, but he'd sold out. He saved himself by going over to the dark side.

I set my books down and spoke to Stenson. "What's up, Jack? Eric do something to you?"

"What's it to you, pizza-face?" Stenson sneered and put Eric down. "You his boyfriend?"

Stevie giggled.

I tried a different approach. I got between Stenson and Eric and said, "Eric, let's go. We've got class."

That's when I got the stomach shot from Jack, and Stevie jumped in to help.

I n Assistant Principal Blackstreet's office, we all stood awaiting our sentences. Roger "Butch" Blackstreet was big, around six-foot-five. He had a head like a bucket, almost no neck, and hands the size of dinner plates. He was also a town legend. He came from an old family, and he'd been Bridgewater High's greatest football player ever. There were still trophies in the school display case with his name on them. He'd been a Marine in Vietnam and won some medals too. He had started at Bridgewater in the seventies as a gym teacher and, of course, football coach.

He was also famous for his temper, which

seemed to get worse as he got older. His players feared him. Three years ago at the homecoming game, he really lost it. His assistants had to hold him back from attacking a player who'd missed a tackle. After that, some parents threatened to sue the school if he wasn't fired as coach. So he was moved into administration. His job was mostly handling discipline problems—including his own. Word was, he still took anger-management classes.

Coach Tyree briefed him on the incident.

"I hope you men are proud of yourselves!" Blackstreet began.

I looked around and saw no men, and no one who seemed to be proud. Stenson was thinking about revenge. Stevie was thinking about his nose. I was thinking about how this would upset Mom. Eric was probably thinking about Mozart. We all knew what would happen.

"This kind of behavior is a disgrace to Bridgewater High," he said. "As of this minute, I'm suspending you all for a week."

Nobody said anything, but Blackstreet stared us down, as if expecting a challenge. "Your parents will be contacted. Making up your class work will be up to you."

Eric sniffled.

"Use this time to think about what you've done," Blackstreet continued. "When you return, I want a written plan from each of you, listing the steps you will take to keep this from happening again. Now get out of here, all of you!

"Except you, Barry. I want to have a few words with you."

The others shuffled out, Stenson staring hard at Eric.

"Have a seat, Mr. Barry," Blackstreet said, pointing to a chair in front of his desk. "I've . . . we've noticed that you've been having some, ah, complexion issues."

"Yes, sir."

"Have you sought medical attention?"

"Yes, sir. Yesterday. I have a prescription."

"It's just that . . . there have been concerns. Did the doctor say if your condition was contagious?"

"He didn't say, sir."

"Well, I guess that doesn't matter now, for the next week at least."

"No, sir."

"Barry, you are one of Bridgewater High's better students. Does that make you think you're above the rules?"

I probably should have said something. Instead I did the absolute wrong thing. I smiled.

In two seconds he was on his feet, jabbing a finger at me. "You think this is funny, Barry? Are you listening to me?"

"No, sir. I mean yes, sir. I'm listening. Not funny."

"Nobody, NOBODY, is above the rules here! Do you understand?"

"Yes, sir."

He took a deep breath. You could see him trying to control himself. At the same time, something very weird was happening to me.

My heart started pounding against my rib cage, as if it were trying to fight its way out. My skin got hot. For the first time I felt pain, searing pain, on my face and my chest. Suddenly I was the one on my feet. An anger I'd never felt capable of had me completely in its power. And powerful it was.

I knew in that second that I was strong enough to snap Blackstreet's neck like a twig.

Without a word, I moved toward him. His eyes were full of surprise. He raised his hands to protect himself.

"Is there a problem in here?" The voice from the doorway belonged to some teacher who had come to see Blackstreet. What he saw was a kid with bad skin and murder in his eyes.

Somehow control returned. My anger burned hot, but it stayed inside. After an awkward silence, Blackstreet spoke in a choked voice. "No problem."

He turned to me: "Go home, Barry. This isn't over."

I walked out into the sunlight. I felt drained, queasy, the way you feel when you come to after fainting.

I could catch the bus home. Before long, my bad day would turn into Mom's bad day.

But my bad day wasn't over yet.

N icholas! Nicholas Barry!"
I was almost home from the bus stop when
I heard Emma Costello calling my name. Does
every neighborhood have a slightly crazy resident?
Someone who knows everyone's business? The one
who calls the cops so often for petty stuff that the
cops don't come anymore? In our neighborhood,
that's Emma.

Emma is in her seventies. She pays me ten
dollars a week to take care of her yard—mow the
grass and weed, trim the bushes twice a year. Before
she retired, she taught English at Saint Philomena,
Bridgewater's Catholic school. Emma's the one who

suggested that poem about the woods for me to memorize. Emma is heavy. She dyes her hair bright orange and always wears screaming red lipstick.

Actually, I like her okay. When I call her slightly crazy, I mean she's a little overboard on a couple of subjects: sin and religion. She'll call the cops when she thinks people are sinning, never mind if they're breaking any laws. Back when Mom's last boyfriend was living with us, she lectured me about Mom's "shacking up" with Vern. Like there was anything I could do. The other thing Emma is big on is the constant battle between the devil and God.

"Nicholas, do you have a moment?"

"Yes, ma'am."

She had something on her mind. "Are you OK? Something going on?" She looked at me carefully.

Crazy or not, Emma was sharp. I gave her the short version of my school day. She shook her head slowly.

"You be careful with Roger Blackstreet," she said. "That whole family has a mean streak. His father was worse. Nothing Butch accomplished was ever good enough."

"I'll watch out. . . . Did you need something?"

"I don't want to embarrass you. You know I care about your welfare, and I want to talk to you about your skin."

Wow. My face seemed to be the topic of conversation wherever I went.

"You've been pure?"

"Ma'am?"

"Your body is a temple of the Holy Spirit, Nicholas."

"I saw a doctor."

"Doctors have their place. What did yours say?"

"He gave me some medicine and said to call him if I didn't get better."

"That's good. But he's a doctor of the body. Have you consulted a doctor of the soul?"

"Ma'am?"

"A priest, Nicholas! A priest!"

"I'm not Catholic."

"The devil craves the souls of young men like you. He is perfectly capable of afflicting their bodies to meet his ends."

"I don't know what . . ."

"Pray, Nicholas! Pray for the Lord's blessing on your skin. He will hear you!"

At this point, I believed we were in "slightly

crazy" territory. "Ma'am, you think my skin problem is a work of the devil?"

"Don't be smart. I didn't say that. Just pray. I will too. And take this."

She reached in her pocket and pulled out a small glass bottle filled with a clear liquid. "This is Lourdes water."

"Lord's water?"

"Lourdes. It comes from a very holy place in France. Sick people from all over the world go there, and many have experienced miracles of healing."

What do I do with it? I wondered. Drink it?

"Keep it with you, Nicholas. And if you feel the presence of the devil, use it to protect yourself."

I took it from her. "Thanks, Miss Costello."

I let myself in the house and heard Toby scampering away. In the kitchen I poured a glass of milk and sat down. I had to figure out how I'd explain things to Mom. By the time I heard her car pull up, I'd decided. She was going to be upset no matter how I told her, so I might as well go with the naked truth.

My luck, though. Just as she walked in the kitchen, the phone rang. She answered it.

"Hello. . . . Yes, I'm Nick's mom."

As she listened, her expression got darker. She looked at me, and her eyes were tired. They seemed to say, Geez, Nick, don't I have enough to deal with already?

"OK, Mr. Blackstreet. I will. Thanks."

She hung up and sighed. "Geez, Nick, don't I have enough to deal with already?"

"Sorry, Mom. It's just a week, and I can keep up with my homework by e-mail."

She shook her head sadly. "You're not hurt?"

"No. I got punched in the stomach, but I'm OK. There was a bully pushing this kid around and . . . "

"It doesn't matter. Mr. Blackstreet said the school has zero tolerance for fighting, period."

She sighed. "Well, I'm going to sit down for a while." She filled a water glass from the sink and headed slowly out to the living room. When you work weekends, Friday nights are nothing special.

I felt bad. Several layers of bad.

    There was my face. I'd stopped looking in the mirror even before I decided to see the doctor. I just wanted to look normal, to be invisible again. I was so tired of being this freak that everyone was either scared of or sorry for. What if this minefield of a face never went away? And even if it did, I'd read enough to know I'd have scars forever.

    And the coldness. At the moment it wasn't so noticeable, just a kind of frost coating my skin. But I knew that sooner or later it would come back like an inner Ice Age. It would turn my bones into frozen iron bars that stuck fast to the wet flesh inside of me.

School. In a week I'd have to go back, and a certain two-hundred-pound gorilla and his pet monkey would be waiting for me.

Then there was Mom. She didn't seem to like her life very much these days. The last time I'd seen her happy was when Vern first moved in. That lasted a couple of months. Then they started arguing. Vern was gone after Christmas, and Mom settled into her old, sad life as if it was what she'd expected all along. I wanted so much for her to feel better. But all I could seem to do was to make her life worse.

And as long as I was having a pity party, I decided I might as well throw in the cat. I believe animals have a special sense about people. They don't have any thinking to complicate their instincts. And now Toby, who used to beg for my attention, was treating me like sour milk.

What I know about feeling bad is this: I can get away into a book or a place that makes me feel good, like the woods or the library, and distract myself for a while. The other thing that helps is work, and fortunately it was my night to make supper. I opened a bag of salad, heated some rolls, and made some chili cheese Hamburger Helper. Mom wasn't too talkative, but she ate seconds. After the dishes I went to my room. I got online and did homework until I felt like I could sleep. Sleep, unfortunately, opens the door for dreams.

In my dream, I was walking alone in my woods at night. The moon was not quite full. It was bright enough, though, that I could see the path that sloped down to the well.

The quiet in the woods wasn't exactly silent. It was more a low hiss, like when you're between radio stations. Over that was the sound of my footsteps scraping the path and the occasional skittering of some small animal in the brush.

And something else. I had the feeling someone was following me. I kept looking over my shoulder, but nothing was there. Someone was walking when I walked, stopping when I stopped. I tried taking a few fast steps, then stopping suddenly. Once I heard an extra step in the dead leaves.

As I came down the path, though, I heard a new sound. It was faint at first, a kind of murmuring. It grew louder as I got in sight of the well. It was clearly a human sound, like the buzz of conversation. Like something I'd heard before. And then the screaming started.

It was the sound I'd heard in my own chest at the doctor's, and it was coming from the well. I should have turned and run, but the well was drawing me closer like a magnet. As I continued forward, the moonlight seemed to change color from white to rust. I felt the coldness coming on. And I smelled something that made me gag, like burning meat.

The well was pulling me to its edge, closer and closer. Suddenly I was there, looking into its depths. I saw water. It was far down, but the moon reflected on its surface was the color of blood. As I watched, the screaming and buzzing grew louder and the reflection began to ripple. Suddenly I was looking not at the moon, but at the most hideous face I had ever seen.

Its skin was red, horribly blistered, and scarred. Its nose seemed to have melted into the hole that had once been its mouth. Its eyes glowed a dull gold. They looked into mine as if the creature knew exactly who I was.

I wanted to look away, but I couldn't move. Not even when I felt cold hands grabbing me from behind. Someone—someone very strong—was lifting me and trying to push me into the well. I grabbed a sharp stone from the crumbling edge of the well and twisted around, striking into the darkness at whatever held me. I pounded it. I could hear shrieks of pain, but I was no match for it. At the last minute I grasped the rim of the well, but it was no use. I felt myself lifted and pushed, and I let go. I screamed as I hit the icy black water.

I woke in what I thought was a cold sweat and turned on the light by my bed. I was cold, no doubt about that. And my T-shirt and shorts were soaking wet. But my right hand was scraped and bleeding. Bits of crumbled stone lay in the scratches. And my clothes—it wasn't sweat they were drenched in. It was blood.

I took off my wet clothes and put them in a laundry bag in my closet, along with the sheets from my bed. As I put on dry things, I noticed an itching on the skin of my chest. Looking down, I saw the scratchy rash the doctor had noticed in his office. The marks were no longer faint, though They were fresh and raised, as if they had just been made by a knife or a claw. They weren't random, either. They looked like writing, like some kind of code.

You wouldn't have thought I could sleep anymore after that. But I dropped off into that black, black place where people go when they're completely exhausted. I woke to the sound of thunder and hard rain, and a banging in the distance. The clock by my bed said 9:00 A.M. Mom would have left for work by now.

Was someone at the door? I was only half-awake when I stumbled into the front room. Through the curtain I saw a tall, thin figure in a hooded robe. Hunched against the storm, he rapped at the door. This wasn't a dream.

I opened the door a crack. The storm was making quite a racket. "What do you want?" I shouted.

And the hooded figure shouted back, "I'm Father Remy Moreau!" He said it like RAY-mee. "I'm a friend of Emma Costello's!"

"What do you want?!"

"I'm here to see Nick Barry!"

I suppose it was risky letting a stranger in, but I did. Father Remy shook himself off, then took off his hood. As he looked at me, his eyes grew wide. "Oh!" he said. "You're Nick."

I'd forgotten that I probably looked just as scary, maybe more, than a guy in a hooded robe. I motioned him toward the kitchen.

In a few minutes we were sitting at the kitchen table. Remy—he asked me to drop the "Father"—was very old, bald with a stubbly white beard. He had dark circles under his eyes that made him look tired. But the eyes themselves were black and quick, like a squirrel's. He seemed like a guy who didn't miss much.

"I'm a priest," he said, as if I hadn't guessed. "I help out at Saint Philomena, saying Mass and teaching religion."

I was looking at his robe. "Oh, I'm a Franciscan priest," he said. "This robe is my habit. I don't usually wear the hood, but the storm . . ."

"You said you were Emma's friend?"

"Ah, yes. Emma was concerned about your spiritual welfare."

"Because of my skin."

Remy looked embarrassed. "Well, your face is . . . startling. But Emma's a good person, even if sometimes she—" The priest shrugged. "What

I did gather was that things might seem a little difficult for you right now. And if you wanted to talk about how you're feeling, I have a special reason to want to listen."

He reached into his robe and pulled out an old, tattered book with a brown cover.

"When I was a young priest, long before you were born, I worked in the neighboring parish, Saint Vincent. And I learned about a young man in your, ah, situation. He . . ."

A hard knocking at the front door interrupted his story. On the step were Dr. Farmer and a blonde woman about his age who looked familiar.

"Hi, Nick," the doctor said. "Sorry to bother you on a weekend, but I . . ." As he looked at me, he couldn't hide his concern. "I may have some more information on your skin problem. Oh, this is my wife, Tara."

The woman put out her hand and smiled at me. "So, you're Nick. You like to hang out at the library, don't you?"

Bingo. Tara was the librarian at the branch nearby. I'd seen her dozens of times before.

"Yeah," I said, shaking her hand. "Look, I've got a pretty weird visitor. Can you come out to the kitchen?" I made coffee for the doc, tea for Tara, and introduced everybody. Then Remy started his story again.

"I was a priest at Saint Vincent over in Baytown in the sixties," he began. "And there was a tragedy at Saint Philomena. A young man about Nick's age, with a serious skin infection. When Emma described Nick, I thought about that young man.

"His name was Luke Todd. When his skin broke out, he became extremely depressed. His schoolmates tormented him. Apparently his girlfriend left him. And his family—he lived alone with his father—didn't suspect how serious his mental state had become.

"I learned this all in the week after young Luke took his own life. His father was devastated with guilt. And so, in a way, was I. I was teaching a class at Saint Philomena, and Luke was in it. But I'd never spoken to him except to call on him in class now and then. I should have noticed."

"How did he die?" Tara asked.

"They found him hanging from a tree in the woods not far from here," Remy said. "I helped the pastor at Saint Philomena with the funeral Mass and the burial. I don't think I've ever been at a sadder service. The only people there were his father, a couple of cousins, and a girl from his school. The father was deeply troubled, as I've said. He'd lost Luke's older brother in Vietnam just a year before. And the girl was very broken up as well."

Remy put his hand on the book. "At the cemetery, Luke's father gave me this—his son's diary. He was afraid that if he kept it, sooner or later he'd read it. And he didn't think he could handle that. He may have been right. Two years later I was offering his funeral Mass.

"Eventually I read the diary. It shows how Luke's depression so separated him from reality that he felt the need to commit his terrible act.

"Luke Todd fell into despair. He couldn't help himself," Remy said sadly. "I thought maybe, by serving as a warning, he could help Nick."

The story Remy was telling seemed pretty out there. I'm not sure I even believed it at the time. But Luke Todd did help me. Just not in the way Remy thought he would.

R emy opened the book, cleared his throat,
and read from the diary of Luke Todd.

10/7/66
*Today is my 16th birthday, and I'm a monster. If I were
a little older, I'd tell people I'd been in Vietnam. My
face looks burned up. In a couple of places you can
almost see bone. No one looks at me. Even the hoods at
school leave me alone, finally. And Amy—Beauty and
the Beast.*

10/10/66

Three weeks ago. Will never forget that day when Amy and I became more than just friends. The first kiss for both of us. We'd been hiking in the woods. I know a place where a circle of stones sits in a clearing, and she seemed as eager to see it as I was to show it to her. We both knew we were in a serious crush. Being together at school over the last couple of weeks had seemed different. We were giddy. We both wondered if the other felt the same, but at the same time we knew that we did.

Finally we were alone together, and we could say what we wanted. We left the woods holding hands. I felt like the king of the universe.

That was then. This is now. I haven't been in school for ten days. Dad's hardly noticed. He works all day. Anyway, he's been a zombie since Brian was killed. The first week Amy called every day. I'd pick up the phone and wait for someone to speak. When I heard her voice, I'd hang up. Once she even came by the house, but I stayed in my room until she went away. I can't stand for her to see me like this. I don't want anyone to see me like this; I don't see a way out.

10/11/66

I don't know anyone I can talk to. Guess that's what diaries are for. But I wonder if I'm just quietly going crazy. "They're coming to take me away! Ha-ha! Ho-ho! Hee-hee!" They played that song a lot last summer. Back then I thought it was funny.

My face looks like hell, but that's just part of it. I'm so cold sometimes! My lips and hands and feet are blue. I tried to feel my heart beating the other day, and it was so slow. And the dreams! That blow-torched face with the yellow eyes staring at me. Is that my face?

10/12/66

The crazy part is this: I feel like something inside me, something that isn't me, is taking me over. Using me. Spending me. For what?

10/13/66

I don't know why I keep going back to that place in the woods. It's like I'm drawn. Like there's something there that wants me to show up. And I'm starting to stutter. I'll just be talking to myself—yeah, like a crazy person—and I can't get the words out. It's like other words are trying to come out at the same time and there's a kind of verbal traffic jam. Once in a while the other words will slip out. They don't make any sense. But they come out loudly, like they'd been bottled up for a long time.

There's a kid at church with some kind of problem. Every now and then, during Mass, he'll just yell out a swear word. Everyone pretends they don't hear. In school a couple of months ago, we saw a film about people speaking in tongues. They seemed to be babbling to me. But Fr. Remy said they believed the sounds they were making came from God. I wonder if the devil could make someone speak in tongues?

What's happening to me?

10/15/66
As I'm writing this, I'm in more pain than I thought was possible. Not physical pain. Worse. I'm sick of heartbreak, of feeling it, of causing it.

Yesterday, I went to the woods again, for reasons I don't understand. Back to the circle of stones. Except this time someone was there. Amy seemed to be meditating. Or praying. I should have turned back right then, but the place was pulling me. When I got within twenty feet of her, I said her name. She jumped a little and turned toward me. Her mouth fell open. There was a second of silence while she tried to understand what she was seeing, and then she let out a scream. I will never, ever allow that scream to happen again. There is no pain worse than causing pain to someone you love. I covered my face, turned, and ran away as fast as I could. Amy kept screaming. Was she calling me? I didn't stop to listen. My fault, my fault.

10/16/66
This person (?) inside of me who wants to take me over: I've started calling him Al. I don't like Al. He's angry and violent. I'm in his way, and yet he needs me. Al is the one who interrupts when I speak. Al is the one who takes me to horrible places when I dream.

I've felt him working on my mind and my body. Yesterday, Dad said something about some chore I hadn't done—as if he has a right to criticize—and Al wanted to kill him. Not just a temper flare. Al had a time, place, and weapon in mind. And I could feel in my muscles the kind of pleasure Al would take in beating my father to a bloody mess. Al needs my body and my will. Every day he seems a little closer to getting what he wants. But I know a way to stop him.

10/17/66
Another night of Al's dreams. I know now that they're Al's, not mine. Fire—there's always fire and always

screaming and always the smell of flesh burning. But this morning I feel better than I have in a long time. Al, you look like toast, and today you are. Dad, Amy, I'm sorry. I love you both.

Remy closed the diary. No one had anything to say, but Tara had tears on her cheeks. I was freaking out inside, but I didn't say anything. Finally, the priest broke the silence.

"Obviously, Luke's affliction drove him mad. The day of this last entry was the day he hanged himself."

"All because of a skin problem?" Tara asked.

"It would seem so," Remy replied. "Although there was something strange about that."

"What?"

"When they cut him down, Luke's skin was perfectly clear."

N o scars?" Doc Farmer asked.

"Nothing," Remy said. "Except where the rope was."

Tara looked at me. "Nick, does any of this sound like what you've been feeling?"

Sometimes you're so full that nothing can come out. I tried. "Yeah. The clearing and the round stone wall—I know where that is. The coldness and the dreams. And the anger that seems to come from nowhere."

"Nick," the doctor said, "the reason I came today was because I got a call from my dermatologist friend. He's not sure you have acne. He says your skin looks more like what he's seen in patients who've been burned."

I flashed on the face in the well.

Remy was getting up from the table. "I have a Bible study in thirty minutes," he said. "May I bless you, Nick?" He put his hands on my forehead and my face—an act of courage for some—and said some Catholic stuff. Then he left.

Now there were three of us.

"Doctor—" I began.

"You can call me Zach."

"What does your friend think about my skin?"

"He's concerned," Zach said. "In rare cases, acne develops into a spreading infection that actually eats the flesh. It can be fatal." I must have looked pretty scared. "I wouldn't worry yet. It's really, really rare, and Ron has only seen a photo. But he'll be in Bridgewater next week. He'd be glad to look at you. No charge.

"It's funny, though, that he should mention burn wounds. Burn victims often die from hypothermia— from coldness. Their system is shocked, and they can't maintain their body temperature. It's strange. You have burns without pain, but with some of the symptoms of a burn victim. I wonder . . ."

His cell phone went off. (Coldplay, "Viva La Vida.") He looked at the phone, said he'd be back in a minute, and headed out to the living room.

Tara took a sip of her tea. "So, Nick, what are you reading these days?"

"Not much," I said. "A couple of weeks ago I started a Stephen King book, but . . ."

"Now you have enough scary stuff going on in real life?"

I nodded.

"Can you tell me about it?"

So I talked about the fight at school and the dream I'd had the night before. I watched her eyes for that look that says, *Uh-oh, freaky, sorry I asked.* But all I saw was kindness and concern. When I was through, she didn't say anything at first. Then she reached out her hands and took both of mine.

Just then the doc returned. "Sorry," he said. "That was Bob, a friend at the hospital. We were supposed to play racquetball this afternoon, but he has to cancel. Things got crazy in a hurry at the hospital. They brought in a kid this morning, and now the place is crawling with police."

He seemed to think of something. "Nick, don't you go to Bridgewater High?"

"Yeah."

"Hang on a second." The doc texted something and waited. The reply was quick. "Nick, do you know a kid named Stenson? John Stenson?"

"Jack? Yeah, I know who he is."

"He's the one they brought into the hospital this morning."

"Jack?"

"Or what was left of him."

We turned on the TV. A reporter was on the scene, standing in front of County Hospital.

". . . in a bizarre attack that has left the youngster clinging to life," she was saying. "We have Sheriff Sean Brady with us. Sheriff, what can you tell us about this brutal incident?"

Sheriff Brady was graying, with one of those bellies you see on movie cops.

"Well, the boy's parents called 911 around nine this morning. They were very upset. The victim was in his room, unconscious. There was a lot of blood."

"What did you see when you arrived at the scene?"

"The victim had lost a great deal of blood, as I said. He had numerous wounds, especially to the face and neck. He was breathing but not responding."

"What kind of wounds did he have, Sheriff?"

"I won't speculate on that at this time. The doctors will help us make that determination."

"Did the victim's family see or hear anything unusual before they discovered the boy?"

"We're still interviewing the family. It's a difficult time for them."

"We can only imagine! Thank you, Sheriff. Once again, a Bridgewater teenager was rushed to County Hospital this morning, the apparent victim of a vicious assault. . ."

I turned off the TV. Doc Farmer's expression was grim. "I heard he lost half his blood. He was in shock when the paramedics got there."

"Did Bob say anything about his injuries?" Tara asked.

"He was beaten and cut. Repeatedly. With

what, they don't know. Bob said his face was unrecognizable."

After a silence, Tara said, "OK, Nick, we need to get going. You have Zach's number. Call us anytime, all right? I'll check in with you on Monday." Then she gave me a long hug.

I walked out with them. The rain had stopped. Just as we got to their car, I heard a familiar voice.

"Nicholas!"

It was Emma. She'd probably been watching the house for hours. We waited while she hurried over. "You've had visitors this morning!"

"Hello, Miss Costello," Tara said.

Emma squinted at Tara a moment, then she exclaimed, "Tara Kelly! You were a freshman in my last year at Saint Philomena!"

"That's right," Tara smiled.

"Are you still a good Catholic girl? I heard you'd married a doctor."

Tara introduced her to Zach.

"Your friend the priest was here too," I said, though I was sure she knew already.

"Father Remy, yes. Was he comforting, Nicholas?"

"Well, he told us about a Saint Philomena kid back in the sixties who hanged himself."

"Luke Todd," Emma murmured, shaking her head sadly. "He was in my tenth grade class."

"You knew Luke?" Tara asked.

"I made it a point to know all of my students," Emma said proudly.

"Did Luke have a girlfriend?" Tara asked. "Someone named Amy?"

"Well," Emma recalled, "they tried not to be obvious about it. But I don't miss too much." She smiled. "They were really darling together."

"Do you know what became of Amy?"

"I do. After Luke . . . passed away, Amy Plasse— that was her name—became very devout. When she graduated, she joined the Sisters of the Holy Blood. Their cloister is out in the country, north of Baytown."

I didn't know the word. "Cloister, ma'am?"

"Sisters in a cloister stay in one place all their lives," Emma explained. "They devote themselves to constant prayer."

Tara looked at me. "Nick, I'm going to give the sisters a call. Maybe we can go out there tomorrow. I feel like the more we know about Luke Todd, the more we'll know about what's going on with you."

The Farmers drove off and Emma went home. I went back in the house and tried to process all that had happened in the last twenty-four hours. The dream. Luke Todd. The attack on Stenson. Tara's hug as she left.

I jumped a little when the phone rang. I looked at the caller ID. It was the Sheriff's Department.

I waited until the phone stopped ringing and then checked the message. The recorded voice was the same as the one from TV, Sheriff Brady himself. Nicholas Barry, please call my office about an important matter, etc. I erased it. If Mom got that call, she'd freak.

And then, just as she was pulling up, the phone rang again. It was Tara.

"Nick, I called the cloister. Amy Plasse is Sister Marie now. It's all right for us to make a short visit tomorrow afternoon. Can I get you at one?"

"Sure."

"Are you all right?"

"Yeah. Uh, my mom just came in."

"OK, see you tomorrow."

"Who was that?" Mom asked.

"Um, the library. I've got a book overdue."

Mom had brought home pizza. So much for fighting zits with healthy food. But her mood was OK. After a dish of ice cream, she headed for her room. "Long day, Nick, and an early morning tomorrow. I'm turning in. Don't forget to lock up."

I did the dishes and put out some food for Toby. I could feel him watching me from a safe distance, from one of those places cats find to make themselves invisible. Why did he hate me these days?

Night was falling, as it always does, even when it's the last thing you want. I wished I could talk to someone. I almost tried Tara, but it was getting late. I'd see her tomorrow, anyway. This having-a-friend thing was new, but I could already see how much I needed it.

I was beat. You'd have thought I'd been chopping wood all day. But I fought sleep. No more dreams, I prayed. No more dreams. God always answers prayers, Emma had told me once. It's just that sometimes his answer is no. Tonight was one of those times.

I was in the woods again, heading for the well. I could see a red glow in the sky over the clearing. As I got closer, the high-pitched screaming began again. I looked ahead to see the well glowing blood red, as if it were brimming with lava. Down into the clearing I went. Despite the fiery pit not twenty feet from me, I was desperately cold. The sounds of tortured people seemed to be coming from all around me, and I looked up into the trees.

Dead men hung like Christmas ornaments from branches all around the circle. Their bloodshot eyes and black tongues bulged out. Their heads were tilted at impossible angles above their nooses. They moaned and twitched as if they were desperate to get down.

Suddenly there was a roar. Flames shot from the well, three stories into the air. At the top of the column of fire, the scalded face I'd seen the night before grinned at me. It hovered there, roasting like a marshmallow in the flame. The stench of burning flesh was overpowering.

As I turned to run, I bumped smack into Butch Blackstreet. The living corpse of Butch Blackstreet. He had a noose dangling from his hand. He was grinning as he held it out to me, and I could smell his rotten breath. I tried to run around him, but he tackled me to the ground. He had long nails that cut like knives and rotten yellow teeth that snapped at my face. Somehow I got my hands around his throat and squeezed as hard as I could. Something snapped. The creature went limp, and I woke up.

I lay for a long time in the shadows of my room. I craved a few minutes more in this "safe" place, between the sadness of my world and the horrors of my dreams.

My arms hurt, and the skin on my chest burned. Finally I leaned over and turned on the lamp by my bed. The first thing I saw was a map of deep, bleeding scratches, like claw marks, on my extended arm. My other arm was the same.

I carefully took off my shirt. My chest was crisscrossed with the same marks—the "writing"

I had noticed after the last dream shone darkly through.

The clock said 3:30 A.M. I went to the bathroom to wash up, not turning on the light. Something flashed as I bent toward the sink. For the first time in days, I looked into the mirror. My eyes—were they mine?—and teeth glowed red in the dark. The pimples on my face were like dozens of red stars in a night sky. It wasn't a face I recognized. I thought of Luke Todd's words: "Something is taking me over." Now I knew what he meant. That thing in the mirror—it wasn't me.

After I washed up, I went outside. Softly, so I wouldn't wake Mom. The moon was full. At this hour, the neighborhood—even Emma—was asleep. I drank in the quiet. My heart had been pounding when I woke up. Now it gradually slowed to normal. The coldness in my bones was going away.

Then I noticed a dark object on the step. I slipped back into the living room and found one of Mom's lighters by the recliner. I came back and clicked it on over the thing.

It was Toby. He stared blankly into the flame, a small pool of blood by his mouth. His head bent at an odd angle to his body. His neck was broken.

I'm too old to cry, but I lost it when I saw Toby.

I remembered how he used to jump in my lap when I was reading. He'd head-butt my book out of the way so he could snuggle against my chest. Then he'd purr like a lawn mower. I wondered again why he'd been avoiding me for the last weeks.

Mom wouldn't be able to handle this. I went as quietly as I could to the kitchen and got a plastic trash bag, some spray cleaner, and paper towels. After I put Toby in the bag, I cleaned the blood off the step. Then I carried everything to the backyard. In a corner, there's a small shed where we keep yard stuff. I got a shovel and tried not to make any noise while I dug Toby's grave.

After I buried him, I covered the fresh earth with leaves. I didn't know the words to say, but it seemed like it was important to say something. "Toby was a good cat," I whispered to the sky, "a good pet. We loved him. I don't know where he is right now, but please watch over him."

I put the shovel away and returned the other stuff to the kitchen. I washed my hands and went to my room. I lay in the dark for a couple of hours with a sad, sick feeling. Around six I could hear Mom in the bathroom, so I got up and made some coffee and toast.

"Why thanks, Nick," she said. "That's really thoughtful! You're up early." Then she looked at me closely for a second. "You know," she said, "I think your skin may be getting a little better." She looked some more, then shrugged. "Maybe not. I don't know. You look different."

The sheriff's office called two times that

morning. Both times I waited, then deleted the message. Tara showed up at one. I wanted to tell her about Toby and the calls from the Sheriff, but all I said was that I'd had some bad dreams.

The Cloister of the Sisters of the Holy Blood is on a hill about a half hour's drive from Bridgewater. We drove through an iron gate into a huge, rolling park with ponds and groves of trees.

"This estate belonged to Hiram Noble," Tara said. "He was a railroad president in the late 1800s. His widow was Catholic, and when she died in the 1920s, she willed the property to the sisters."

The cloister itself looked like what it had been, according to Tara: a sprawling, three-story stone mansion. We left the car by a sign that said "Visitors' Parking" and buzzed in at the front door.

An old woman wearing a white apron over a long black dress let us in. The front hall was tiled with dark green and white marble in a diamond pattern. A huge oak staircase rose in front of us, and colorful light spilled through a stained-glass window on the landing. Long hallways extended on either side of us.

The woman led us down the hall to the right. We went past portraits of nuns and priests, past a giant statue of Jesus hanging on the cross, and into a small, wood-paneled room. On one wall was a window about chest high. Instead of glass, it was covered with metal grating. By the window were several chairs where Tara and I were directed to sit.

"It's called a grille," Tara whispered. "Sister will speak with us from the other side."

A few minutes later, a light went on behind the grating. A veiled figure sat down on the other side. After my eyes got used to the grille, I could see through it pretty well. The nun looked much younger than she actually had to be. There were no lines in her face, and her expression was calm.

"Hello, I'm Sister Marie."

Tara was introducing us when I remembered my manners. Since my face got bad, I'd worn a baseball cap with the brim down whenever I went out. But now I took it off and looked at the woman who used to be Amy Plasse.

I could hear her gasp. "I'm sorry—" I started.

"No, I'm sorry, Nick," she said. "You just reminded me of someone I knew once."

uke Todd?" Tara asked. "It's actually Luke that we wanted to ask you about."

Sister Marie didn't say anything. She just sat quietly, looking as if she were examining something far away. Finally Tara went on. "I know it was a long time ago. It may be hard to remember . . . ."

"No," Sister Marie said finally. "It's not difficult. I've thought of Luke almost every day of my life since then."

"We wonder," Tara said, "if Nick might be going through some of the same stuff Luke did, all those years ago. Father Remy Moreau showed us Luke's diary, and there are some strange similarities."

"Tell me about it, Nick," the nun said. I told her about my skin, the woods, the dreams—and the face I'd seen in the well.

"Luke called the face—or the person behind the face—Al," Sister Marie said. "If Al has set his sights on you, you need God's help very badly."

"Sister," Tara asked, "why do you think Luke killed himself?"

The nun laughed, but in a sad, knowing way. "Oh, to save the world," she said. "To save me." There was an awkward silence until Sister Marie continued. "Let me tell you a little about Luke," she said. "Did you know he had lost his brother in the war?"

"Brian?" Tara asked.

"Yes. Sometimes I almost wonder if the war that killed Brian killed Luke too. He worshipped his older brother. And after his death, Luke was determined to be a hero just like him. Not in a conceited way, but in a soldierly way. No matter what happened he would protect the weak. All by himself."

"He loved you, Sister," Tara said. "His diary was full of—"

"Oh, I know," the nun interrupted. "And I loved him. Still do. But sometimes—God forgive me—I'm so angry. I would have done anything for him. Anything. And he left me out. I can't tell you how many times I've wondered if things would have turned out differently if he'd just shared what he was feeling with me."

She turned to me. "Nick, if Luke can teach you anything, it's this: Don't go it alone. God loves you, but he uses people to show that love. If anyone loves you, let them in. Let them help you. Don't go it alone! You're not strong enough, and there's no shame in that."

Tara put her arm across my shoulders. "Sister," she said, "I know Luke didn't talk to you in the last days of his life."

"The last time I saw him was in the clearing, by the circle of stones. I went there hoping he might appear. It was our place. But when he did come, he startled me. I screamed. He ran. I kept calling to him, 'Come back! Please!' But he didn't stop.

"That was the last time I saw him alive. But it wasn't the last I heard from him. Can you wait a minute?"

We both nodded and she left. She came back a few minutes later holding a folded paper. "The day he died, Luke mailed me a letter," she said. "When I read it, I'm afraid I cursed him. I had wanted his trust, his love—not a suicide note. It's taken a lot of prayer, but I know now that he was trying to do what he thought his hero brother would have done. Sometimes it still hurts, though. Funny, a teenage crush forty years ago, and yet . . . ."

We waited. "I'll read you what he wrote," Sister Marie said. She put on a pair of glasses. "He starts by talking about us. I'll skip that, if you don't mind." A deep breath.

"'Amy, I expect most people would consider me a nut case. But I know you will believe me when I say that this stuff is supernatural. Something—Al or whatever—but something evil, wants to enter this world. And our place in the woods is some kind of gateway. I think, way back, something bad happened there. I don't think Al will stop, even if he fails with me. There's another world, Amy. Pray to God that it doesn't get into ours!'"

One more time, Sister Marie spoke directly to me: "Nick, I believe Luke is in heaven, despite the manner of his death. If you pray, speak to him. He will help you if he can."

We thanked Sister Marie. On the drive back to Bridgewater, I thought about prayer. I wanted to ask for help, but I wasn't sure I knew how. The way home took us right through Baytown, where there was a traffic jam. Apparently some accident or emergency; we heard sirens everywhere.

When we got back to my street, I spotted Mom's car in the drive. She was home early for some reason. "Tara, drop me off here," I said, a block and a half away.

She pulled over, then leaned across the seat and hugged me. "Come to the library tomorrow," she said. "And remember what Sister said. We're in this together."

I walked to my house. When I opened the door,

Mom came hurrying out of the kitchen. Her eyes were red and full of fear. "Nick!" she cried. "Why is the sheriff looking for you?"

C alm down, Mom, I'll tell you what I know. Let's go to the kitchen." Something about the kitchen. It's a safe place. "Mom, do you remember the fight at school?"

"Of course."

"The kid who punched me was attacked by someone on Saturday. He's in the hospital. I'm pretty sure the sheriff is checking on people who knew the kid, especially people who might have had a problem with him." For Stenson, I thought, that's a long list.

"I got called at work," Mom said like it was my fault. "I had to punch out early."

"Why?"

"I told the sheriff I'd meet him here, with you. He'll be here in half an hour."

"All right," I said, but my mind was racing. It doesn't matter how innocent you are. If the police are after you, part of you feels guilty. Maybe it was also because of the calls I'd erased.

Fifteen minutes later there was a knock at the door. I tried to prepare myself. But it was just Emma.

"Oh, Nicholas!" she wailed. "Have you heard?" My confused look was answer enough.

"Father Remy! His house burned down last night! He died in the fire!"

Emma was sobbing. I didn't know what to do. I hugged her a little. "I'm sorry," I said. But sorrow, to tell the truth, wasn't my first emotion. It was more like panic. What in the world was going on here?

Emma wasn't gone five minutes when the sheriff's car pulled up. Sheriff Brady was with a younger man in uniform, his deputy.

"You're Nick?" the sheriff asked. I nodded.

Mom invited them both into the living room, and we all sat down.

"Nick, you know John Stenson? You've heard about what happened?"

"On TV, yes, sir."

He pulled a little notepad from his jacket. "A couple of people we talked to—Mr. Blackstreet and a student named Steven Furman?—said you and John Stenson fought last week."

"Nick was protecting another boy," Mom said, but the sheriff ignored her.

"Mr. Blackstreet said you'd both been suspended. He also said he thought you were trouble."

I waited for an actual question.

"Where were you on Friday night?"

"I was here at home, sleeping." If you could call it sleep, I thought.

"Did you have any contact with John Stenson after the incident at school?"

"No, sir."

"Sometime on Friday night or early Saturday morning, Mr. Stenson was assaulted." The sheriff watched me carefully as he spoke. "He was hit repeatedly on the face and head with a heavy, sharp object. We haven't found a weapon.

However, doctors say his wounds are consistent with someone who was beaten with a rock or a brick." The sheriff paused, still staring at me intently.

"Mr. Stenson is in a coma. He may have brain damage." I bit my tongue. Why did I keep thinking of wisecracks? This was serious.

"Can I look at your hands, Nick?"

I wasn't sure what my rights were. Wasn't I supposed to ask for a lawyer or something? I waited a second, but I didn't want to seem guilty, so I held them out. The sheriff took my right hand and looked closer.

"How did you get this scrape on your palm?"

I wasn't about to tell anyone about my dream and the struggle by the well. "I don't remember," I said. "Maybe in the fight at school?"

"Roll your sleeves up, son."

My arms still had angry scratches from wrists to elbows. The sheriff looked at Mom. "Ma'am, do you mind if we look around the house? We don't have a warrant, so you can say no. But we'll be careful not to mess the place up."

Mom looked at me. I was about to shrug when I remembered the bloody clothes in my closet. I shook my head.

"I'm sorry," Mom told the sheriff.

He wasn't pleased. "Have it your way. But we will get a warrant to search this place. And don't think about going anywhere or getting rid of any evidence, son. We'll be watching you."

At last, the sheriff and the deputy were gone, at least for now. But Mom was hysterical. "What's going on, Nick?" she cried.

"Mom," I pleaded. "I didn't do anything." I sounded just like every perp on every crime show on TV. What I said was true. But when Mom asked where Toby was, I lied and said I didn't know.

That evening after Mom turned in, I called Tara. I told her what had happened.

"OK, Nick," she said. "I don't think scratches on your arms are enough reason for them to get a search warrant. But they'll be keeping an eye on you until they get more. So just leave everything the way it is. I'm checking out some new information. I'll call you in the morning."

Late that night, I buried the laundry bag and its contents near Toby. Somehow I'd find a way to explain Toby's disappearance to Mom. But right now I had too much other stuff to figure out.

Around noon the next day, Tara called. "Can you come to the library this afternoon? Around four? I want you to meet someone."

I said sure. I was trying to decide what to do until then when I heard someone at the door. Did the sheriff get a warrant after all? I looked through the curtains in the front room. It wasn't the police. It was Blackstreet.

Just the sight of him and my heart started beating in overdrive. I started to feel all prickly along the back of my neck. I went to the door. The assistant principal had his swagger back and a big, evil smile.

"Hey, Barry."

"Why are you here? My mom's working."

"A little defensive, aren't we?" He stretched. "I was just in the neighborhood. My family owns some property out this way, and I check on it now and then. So I thought I'd stop by on my lunch hour and see how you were enjoying your, ah, vacation."

Sure, I thought. The guy's a jerk. But you've met jerks before. Why do you want to kill this one? But the same hatred I'd felt in his office was trying to overcome me. OK, Nick, control yourself.

"I thought we might have a little chat," Blackstreet said, "about your attitude."

"Attitude, sir?"

"Cut the crap, Barry. I could see it in my office. You don't like me. In fact, you hate my guts."

He had that right. When he said "my guts," a picture of me ripping them out flashed into my mind. "I really don't know what you mean," I lied, while I imagined his intestines unraveling.

"Look," he said, his voice getting darker and that finger jabbing again. "Nobody, especially no kid, gives me a face like you did without paying the price. Maybe you think, now that Stenson's a vegetable, that your return to Bridgewater High will be a piece of cake."

I didn't answer.

"Wrong, pal. Your attitude needs some fixing, and I'm going to make sure that happens."

I was beginning to understand something. The anger rising inside of me wasn't exactly mine. It was Al's. Why did Al hate this guy so much? I didn't have a clue. But anger is as much physical as mental, and the body channeling Al's anger was mine. I had never felt so split in two. Part of me was a murderer. Part of me was trying to stop a murder.

"There it is again," Blackstreet smirked. "That look. Well, we could just mix it up here, you think? But I guess, for me, that would be what they call a bad career move."

For you, I thought—or Al thought—that would be an express ride to hell.

"Well," he pretend-sighed, "I don't want to wear out my welcome. I just wanted to let you know how much I'm looking forward to our next, ah, encounter."

Blackstreet turned and headed away. Suddenly I heard a voice, like a growl, coming from my mouth. To this day, I don't know what I said, but I know what it meant to convey—pure and primal hatred.

I got to the library at four and found Tara at the desk. "Hi, Nick! Look, I've been online for the last couple of days looking for information about your well. It turns out there's somebody local who might be able to help."

She showed me to a cubicle in back where the staff had their offices. Sitting there was a tall, skinny, older man wearing a bow tie and a tweed jackct. It was my first look at Lester Smythe, PhD.

When he saw my face, I got the wide-eyed thing. Then he jumped up and extended his hand. "Hello, hello!" he said. "You must be Nick."

His accent was British, or Australian, like that lizard on the car insurance commercials. He introduced himself, complete with initials.

"Dr. Smythe is a professor of anthropology at Noble College," Tara said.

"Anthropology?"

"The study of old civilizations," Dr. Smythe informed me. "How people lived in the past, how they got along with each other, what they believed about their existence."

"Like, say, the Egyptians?"

"Yes, like that. Although my own specialty is regional Native American civilization: the history and customs of indiginous people in this area."

"Do you know about the stone walls that go all through the woods around here?" I asked. "I've always wondered if Indians made them."

"Excellent question!" Dr. Smythe exclaimed. "In fact, those walls were built by colonial farmers in the late 1700s to mark their property."

"When I was searching, I came across a paper Dr. Smythe published in 2002," Tara said. "I think it has to do with your well."

Dr. Smythe wanted to know exactly where the circle of stones was located. When I told him, his eyes lit up.

"Well done, Tara!" he said. "That's the very place I wrote about! I enlisted the help of a couple of grad students, and the Blackstreets allowed us to study—"

"Did you say Blackstreets?" I interrupted.

"Yes, the Blackstreet family has owned that land for centuries. In any case, the artifact you describe as a well is very old, much older than the walls. If you examine the stonework, it's quite different. It served some sort of religious purpose for the native people here. It's not a well, though. It's a fire pit of some kind."

"But in 1656, something very ugly happened on that spot. That winter, everyone in this part of the country was starving. Five members of a local tribe raided a settlement nearby. They stole food, and they also killed and scalped eight settlers who were taking over their hunting grounds. Can you guess what happened next?"

"The settlers fought back?"

"Yes, but not against the native peoples. There was someone they hated more. The settlers referred to them as the Outcasts. They were families who had come to the New World on the same ships as the Puritan settlers. But they weren't Puritan. They weren't even British.

"Crossing the Atlantic, the Puritans weren't particular about who came with them, as long as they could pay their way. But the Puritans nurtured a deep, religion-fueled hatred of these people even as they accepted their money."

"Who were they?"

"Ah, now that's very interesting. Some scholars think they might be related to the Roma people, who used to be called Gypsies. I think they might have been Zoroastrians, perhaps from Persia—modern Iran. The Puritans would have considered that religion and its practices not just wrong, but an insult to God."

"The Puritans were pretty hard core, weren't they?" I asked.

"That's one way to put it. The Puritans quickly turned on these people when they settled in this area, forcing them to live apart. That wasn't enough, though. We're talking about a time when some Christian religions believed that heresy should be punished by death. The Puritans bided their time, for generations. But when the Indians killed those settlers, they saw an opportunity."

"First of all they raided the Outcast settlement and rounded up all the men. Then they announced a trial on charges of heresy and witchcraft."

"That's bogus. They couldn't just lie about them and then kill them."

"A very intelligent response, Nick. The Puritans did not want to be accused of a lynching. So they took advantage of the local anger about the Indian raid. At a key moment in the trial, a band of settlers disguised as Indians descended on the Outcasts. The onlookers pretended to be horrified. But they didn't lift a finger to help and, of course, were never threatened themselves.

"First, the accused were held down and skinned. Alive. It's said that the screaming could be heard a mile away. Next, they were strung from the trees by their necks until they strangled."

I could hear the screaming from my dreams.

"Then the skinned bodies of the hanged were cut down and thrown into the fire pit. Wood was thrown on top of them and set aflame. It's said the column of flame rose as high as the trees."

I saw the fire from my dream.

"The point was to kill them in a way that made it look like the Indians did it. Before the bodies of the hanged were burned, some of the settlers took . . . souvenirs. Scalps, ears, teeth, pieces of skin. There are even reports that one of the Outcasts, a sort of leader, was cannibalized."

As Dr. Smythe spoke, I felt anger rising inside me. Not just my own anger, but someone else's. A powerful bitterness that raged for revenge. The coldness came over me, and my chest burned. Then I heard a deep voice mutter strange words from my mouth. Tara gasped, and Dr. Smythe shrank back in his chair and stared at me as if I had two heads.

"Do you know what you just said?"

"That was my voice?"

"Not your voice, but coming from your mouth, in a language very few people know today. You said, 'We return from death to bring death!'"

A language very few people know. I thought about the marks on my chest. It was worth a try.

"Dr. Smythe," I said, lifting my shirt, "do these marks mean anything to you?"

He looked confused for a moment, then his eyes grew wide. "God save us!" he whispered. "It says, 'Skin for Skin.'"

Iara grabbed my arm.

"There's something else though," Lester said.

"What's that?"

"It's backward. As if it had been written by someone inside you."

None of us knew what to say next. Finally Dr. Smythe stood up. "Nick, Tara, I need to get going. I have an evening class to teach. If I can help either one of you—Tara, you have my number."

After he left, I told Tara I thought Luke Todd had been right. Al had used him. And now Al was somehow using me—my skin—to get into the world and take revenge.

"The problem," I said, "is that I don't know how to fight him. How do you fight someone who is inside of you?"

Tara's face clouded over.

"Don't worry. I'm not going to hang myself."

Her eyes teared up and she hugged me, hard. "You've got that right," she said.

"Tara, the only times I've seen Al outside of me have been in the woods. I need to go there."

"Absolutely not! That place belongs to him. It's evil!"

I took her hands. "What do we want to happen?"

"We want Al to leave you alone!"

"What about the rest of the world? If Al gets into the world, through me . . . Tara, you can't imagine how crazy angry he is."

"Nick, we save you first. What was it Sister Marie said about Luke wanting to save the world?"

"Al will hurt people. I think he already has."

When someone attacks you, you have two choices. You can fight back, or you can just hope the attacker will go away. Al wasn't going away. I had to do something.

Just then Tara's cell phone rang. (Alicia Keys, "No One.") "That was Zach," she said when she was finished. "John Stenson died."

It was so strange. Three days ago I'd felt this guy's fist in my stomach. Now he was gone from this world. But Tara had a more immediate concern.

"Nick, you're a murder suspect now. They'll arrest you."

One more reason to head for the woods. They wouldn't look for me there. But first there was something I needed at home.

I asked Tara if she'd drive me there. Some serious weather was moving in. It was 5:30 P.M. and people already had all their lights on. As Tara dropped me off she said, "Come to the library first thing in the morning. We'll figure something out. Together."

"OK," I lied. I hoped she'd forgive me.

Mom was in the kitchen. "I've got lasagna in the oven," she said, as she filled her glass from the wine bottle. "Should be ready in half an hour." She turned toward the living room, where the TV was already on. "Where's the cat?"

"Mom," I said, "I'm sorry."

She stopped and looked surprised. "Sorry? For what?"

"For causing you all these problems. And I'm sorry—Toby got hit by a car and I buried him. I was afraid to tell you. Thanks for standing up to the sheriff."

She set down her glass. "Nick, you're my only son. I love you. Even if you had done something—and I know you didn't—even so, I'd love you." She walked across the kitchen and we hugged.

"Thanks, Mom," I said. "Everything will be OK." Was that another lie?

Mom headed toward the TV. I grabbed what I needed from my room. My hand was on the back door when I heard a knock at the front, then voices.

"Ma'am . . . warrant . . . murder."

The sheriff worked fast. I didn't wait for the end of the conversation.

Outside, the wind was swirling. There were occasional flashes in the sky. No thunder yet, but a storm was definitely approaching. I dodged between houses. At one point, I ducked behind a hedge when I saw a police cruiser drive by very slowly. In ten minutes I was in the woods.

All around me the tree branches were waving. The wind came in long sighs, while the leaves scraped against each other. I started to hear thunder in the distance.

I could feel a kind of storm brewing inside me
as well. Al was wide awake, and he grew stronger
as I approached the clearing. His fantasies of
revenge played like a widescreen movie in
my head: scenes of torture I could never have
invented, blood and screams and fire.

As I neared the clearing, the coldness set in.
I felt the magnetic pull of the well. The storm's
strength grew along with Al's. Rain started to spit,
and jagged lightning streaked the sky. Thunder
cracked.

I was ten feet from the well when Al's hands
appeared at the rim. I watched in horror as a naked,
seven-foot-tall man, glowing red, climbed out of
the well. He stood before me, his arms folded,
laughing. He was hairless, his entire body charred
and blistered. His features were twisted and
sagging as if they had melted and refrozen. He was
no Outcast. He was the king of hell.

Al said nothing, but as I watched he glowed
a brighter and brighter red, like molten metal.
The raindrops hissed and steamed as they fell
on him. And the brighter he became, the colder

I felt, colder than ever before. I was shivering uncontrollably in the pelting rain. My face was burning and my chest felt heavy and sore as if I'd been beaten.

ammit, Nick, what do you think you're doing?" a female voice boomed.

How long had I been standing in the clearing? The storm was gone. It was dark. I felt incredibly tired. Emptied. But I could still think. *Tara,* my mind told me.

I was able to turn, slowly. Zach was behind her.

"I'm sorry," I whispered.

They had brought a blanket. Tara was putting it around my shoulders when suddenly she stared past me and gasped. "Zach!"

I didn't have to wonder what she saw. I could

feel Al approaching. As he stepped forward, Tara screamed. And then, literally, all hell broke loose.

There was a roaring, crackling sound, and the smell of burning meat. Flames shot up from the well and, one by one, thirty men climbed out. They were on fire. Many were missing ears or hands or scalps. Their necks were mangled, and they screamed in pain and anger as they formed a circle around the clearing.

Then, at a signal from Al, the circle began to close. The flames in the well rose higher as the burning corpses got closer. Al stood outside the circle now, laughing in triumph.

As the circle of fiery men closed in on us, an odd, sad thought passed through my head. Since this whole skin thing started, my life had actually gotten better in some ways. I'd stood up to Stenson. Emma—yeah, she could be a pain, but she cared about me. In Tara, for the first time, I had a real friend. And tonight I realized that Mom really saw me, and loved me. Does this happen to everyone, that they notice the good things in their lives just before they're about to lose them?

We all retreated toward the well as the heat from

the dead men and the stench of their smoldering bodies became unbearable. Is there any death more horrible than burning? People have been known to leap from flaming skyscrapers to avoid fire.

The Outcasts were just about on top of us when we all heard a deafening explosion. It came from a shotgun. A shotgun wielded by Butch Blackstreet. The noise got the attention of Al and his ghouls, who stopped advancing.

"What the hell is going on here?" Blackstreet yelled.

No one said a word. Blackstreet looked confused. "I get a call that my woods are burning and . . ."

He spotted me through the flames. "Barry!" he roared. "What are you doing here?"

I didn't say anything. But Al took a step past me toward Blackstreet. And another.

"You're trespassing!" the assistant principal shouted. "Setting fires on my property!" He raised his shotgun.

But as he looked to aim, Blackstreet stopped mid-position. He finally seemed to take in the horror before him. His jaw gaped open. "What the hell—?"

Before Blackstreet could run away, Al signaled the fiery corpses. They broke their circle and wheeled around the terrified man.

Blackstreet fired his gun. His bullets ripped through the dead men's flesh, but they kept coming toward him. In an instant he was swarmed by burning corpses. They clawed at his body and grabbed for his throat.

Yesterday, I—or Al inside me—would have fantasized about a sight like this. But now, watching my revenge play out, the rush was gone. I felt no anger at all. What happened in 1656 wasn't Blackstreet's fault. Now I felt his pain and fear wash over me.

That's when a voice, loud enough to carry over the Outcasts' cries, stopped everything. It was mine.

"Stop!"

The Outcasts, who had been intent on slaughtering Blackstreet, turned to look at me. Al turned too. I heard Tara behind me: "Nick! Don't!"

I looked at her, and she must have seen something in my face. In the next second, she was at my side, and Zach at hers.

I reached into my pocket to retrieve what I'd gone home to get: Emma's holy water. I opened it, splashed some on all three of us and took a step toward Al. What did I have to lose?

"You use people," I said. "You make people hate each other until they kill. Why?"

Al laughed, and without speaking, signaled his ghouls to attack. But nothing happened. The Outcasts stood quietly, watching him.

"You didn't help these men," I said to Al. "You caused the hate that killed them! And now you're using their hate to cause more killing!"

I faced the Outcasts: "Is this your boss? He doesn't care about you. Your families cared about you. You cared about each other. He only cares about pain!"

With an ear-splitting war cry, Al ordered his slaves to advance. And they came. But it was Al they were after. As they surrounded him, I saw Blackstreet run off into the woods. The men danced around Al, closer and closer, like a flaming saw.

He roared in pain as they hooked their fingers in his eyes and tore off his flesh. He bellowed curses as they lifted him over their heads and carried him toward the pit. Just before they threw him in, Al looked straight at me and pointed his finger. As if to say, "I know who you are. This isn't over."

Then he was gone. The fire in the well followed him. And one by one, like candle flames, the burning Outcasts flickered out. Thirty innocent men had been abused in life and used in death. Now their souls were finally free.

The next voice I heard was Tara's, "Nick!" She was crying.

"It's all right," I said.

"Your skin, Nick. It's clear! Zach, look!"

Tara, Zach, and I didn't know what to say. We hugged each other close and then started our walk home. The first light of morning was turning the blackness to gray. We were near the edge of the woods when we saw flashlight beams and heard dogs barking. They were police dogs, and a search party led by Sheriff Brady wasn't far behind.

There never was a murder charge, as it turned out. There really wasn't any evidence. Traces of blood in my closet "were compatible" with Jack Stenson's. But the bloody fingerprints they found in his room weren't mine. The prints in Stenson's room also matched prints found at Father Remy's house in Baytown. The police had decided that the fire that killed the priest was arson. They're still looking for a suspect in both crimes. I don't think they'll find him in this world.

After my suspension, I went back to school.

Blackstreet was on a "leave of absence," so the principal accepted my written plan for staying out of trouble. Stevie Furman had transferred to Saint Philomena.

I wrote a letter to Sister Marie. I wasn't specific, but I thanked her for her time and advice, and told her I would pray for her and Luke.

While Emma might have believed what happened if I told her, I only thanked her for the holy water. I was sure it was important in clearing up my complexion, I said.

Mom seems happier lately. We're getting along OK. She's happy about my new job helping at the library after school.

I haven't had any nightmares since that night in the woods, but I haven't gone back to the clearing. I don't think Al is dead. I don't think evil is ever dead. But neither is good. I just hope goodness will always be ready and willing to fight. I know Al will.

Everything's fine in Bridgewater. Really . . .

Or is it?

Look for these other titles from the
Night Fall collection.

MESSAGES FROM BEYOND

Some guy named Ethan Davis has been texting Cassie. He seems to know all about her—but she can't place him. He's not in Bridgewater High's yearbook either. Cassie thinks one of her friends is punking her. But she can't ignore the strange coincidences—like how Ethan looks just like the guy in her nightmares.

Cassie's search for Ethan leads her to a shocking discovery—and a struggle for her life. Will Cassie be able to break free from her mysterious stalker?

THAW

A July storm caused a major power outage in Bridgewater. Now a research project at the Institute for Cryogenic Experimentation has been ruined, and the thawed-out bodies of twenty-seven federal inmates are missing.

At first, Dani Kraft didn't think much of the breaking news. But after her best friend Jake disappears, a mysterious visitor connects the dots for Dani. Jake has been taken in by an infamous cult leader. To get him back, Dani must enter a dangerous, alternate reality where a defrosted cult leader is beginning to act like some kind of god.

THE CLUB

The club started innocently enough. Bored after school, Josh and his friends decided to try out an old game Sabina had found in her basement. Called "Black Magic," it promised the players good fortune at the expense of those who have wronged them. Yeah, right.

But when the club members' luck starts skyrocketing—and horror befalls their enemies—the game stops being a joke. How can they end the power they've unleashed? Answers lie in an old diary—but ending the game may be deadlier than any curse.

THE PROTECTORS

Luke's life has never been "normal." How could it be, with his mother holding séances and his half-crazy stepfather working as Bridgewater's mortician? But living in a funeral home never bothered Luke. That is, until the night of his mom's accident.

Sounds of screaming now shatter Luke's dreams. And his stepfather is acting even stranger. When bodies in the funeral home start delivering messages to Luke, he is certain that he's going nuts. As he tries to solve his mother's death, Luke discovers a secret more horrifying than any nightmare.

UNTHINKABLE

Omar Phillips is Bridgewater High's favorite local teen author. His Facebook fans can't wait for his next horror story. But lately Omar's imagination has turned against him. Horrifying visions of death and destruction come over him with wide-screen intensity. The only way to stop the visions is to write them down. Until they start coming true . . .

Enter Sophie Minax, the mysterious Goth girl who's been following Omar at school. "I'm one of you," Sophie says. She tells Omar how to end the visions—but the only thing worse than Sophie's cure may be what happens if he ignores it.